My Nursery Story Book

For Emily Hope, Alice Lily Hope,
and their oak tree

My Nursery Story Book

Ian Beck

BARNES
&NOBLE
BOOKS
NEW YORK

Originally published in 1998 as
The Oxford Nursery Story Book

This edition published by Barnes & Noble, Inc.,
by arrangement with Oxford University Press.

1999 Barnes & Noble Books

ISBN 0-7607-1942-X

99 00 01 02 03 04 MC 9 8 7 6 5 4 3 2 1

Printed in Spain

Contents

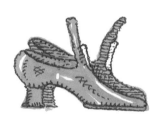

Jack and the Beanstalk

O nce upon a time, when there was still magic, there lived a boy called Jack. He lived with his mother in a little house on their farm. They were very poor, and the only possession they had left was Daisy the cow. Daisy was a very nice, but very old, cow and was the only real friend that Jack had. But one day Jack's mother said that it was no good, there was nothing left to eat, he must take Daisy to market and sell her or else they would starve.

The next morning Jack set off with Daisy, to walk to market. His mother waved them goodbye, and said, 'You make sure you get a good price, you know what a fool you are.'

Jack was sad to be selling Daisy, so he walked very slowly, hoping to be too late for the market. After a while they met an old man walking in the opposite direction. He was a very odd man; he was bent almost double and wore strange clothes, all colored in green.

'Good morning, boy,' said the old man. 'What a fine cow. Where are you taking her?'

'I must take her to market and sell her, for we are very poor,' said Jack with a sigh.

'I never saw such a splendid animal,' said the old man. 'I should like to buy her myself.' And with that he reached into his green purse, and pulled out five beans.

Now, Jack had hoped for some gold coins. 'Those are beans,' he said. 'I couldn't sell Daisy for beans.'

'Ah,' said the old man, 'but these are magic beans. Plant these in your garden by moonlight and you will see.'

Jack was a trusting boy and he sold Daisy to the strange old man for the five magic beans.

His mother called him a fool. It was worse than she had feared, she said, now they would really starve. But Jack believed the old man, and that night, under the full moon, he planted the five beans.

His mother woke him early with a clout on the head. 'Now look what you've done!' she cried.

Jack hopped out of bed, and into the garden. Those beans really had been magic. Where he had planted them there now stood an enormous beanstalk with huge leaves. It stretched up into the sky and beyond the clouds. Jack saw at once a chance for adventure and perhaps even a fortune. Straightaway he began to climb.

Up and up he went, higher and higher, until he found himself above the clouds and in a different world.

Ahead of him stretched a long twisty road turning among the clouds and at the end of the road stood a huge castle. Jack walked up to the castle and climbed the steep steps to the door.

'Whoever lives here must be a giant,' said Jack to himself. He slipped into the castle through a crack in the door and found himself in a vast room with a fire blazing and a big table with legs made of tree trunks.

By the table was a wooden cage and in the cage Jack could see a fat white goose tied by a rope. 'Honk! Help me escape from here,' said the goose, 'and you will never be poor again, for I am a magic goose.'

Now Jack had good reason to believe in magic; the old man had been right about the beans after all. 'All right,' said Jack. 'I'll have you out of there in no time.'

But as he started to pull on the bars there came a sound like thunder,

BOOM . . .

BOOM . . .

BOOM,

and with it a voice low and loud . . .

Fee Fi Fo Fum
I smell the blood of a British man
Be he alive or be he dead
I'll grind his bones to make my bread.

'Quick,' said the goose, 'here comes the giant. Now hide where you can.' So Jack climbed up to the table top and hid behind a huge egg-cup. The door crashed open and in walked a terrible giant. He sat at the table, banged down his great fist, and laughed, 'Ho, ho, ho . . . where is my lovely goosey-goosey?'

The giant leaned down and picked up the cage and the goose. He pulled open the door, sat the poor goose in the middle of the table, and boomed out, 'Lay, goose, lay.' And the goose let out a sad 'honk', and laid an egg.

The giant picked up the egg and laughed again, 'Ho, ho, ho', and then carefully put the egg in the egg-cup. It was an egg of solid gold. Jack stared—it really was a magic goose. 'Lay, goose, lay,' said the giant again, and again the goose laid a golden egg, and so on until it had laid six eggs in all. Jack watched as the giant gradually fell asleep with a big smile on his face.

Jack crept out from behind the egg-cup and quickly untied the rope from the goose's neck. 'Climb on my back,' said the goose. And with Jack on her back she flew up and out of the castle window.

The flap of her wings woke the giant with a start, and as they flew down the road towards the beanstalk, the giant blundered after them, calling out, 'Goosey-goosey, come back.'

Jack hurled himself down the beanstalk, while the goose flew down beside him. But the giant started to climb down the beanstalk as well and his weight caused it to sway this way and that. Jack saw his mother at the bottom of the beanstalk and he called out to her to fetch the axe. As soon as Jack reached the ground he took the axe and chopped, until the beanstalk and the giant crashed to the ground. The giant, being so heavy, made such a hole that he fell right through the earth and was never seen again.

When Jack's mother saw the huge goose she was cross again. 'Whatever is that gert ugly bird?' she said. 'We can hardly feed ourselves let alone a gert thing like that.'

'It's a magic goose,' said Jack. 'Just you watch this. "Lay, goose, lay," ' he said to the goose, and patted it kindly on the head. The goose let out a happy 'honk' and laid a single golden egg, as it did once a year every year from then on. And so Jack, and his mother, and the goose, lived happily in comfort for the rest of their days.

Little Red
Riding Hood

Once upon a time, in a far-away place, there lived a girl who was called 'Little Red Riding Hood'. Everyone called her that because she always wore a red cape with a hood that her grandmother had made for her. She lived with her mother in a neat white house on the edge of a deep dark forest.

One morning her mother called her. 'Your granny isn't feeling very well,' she said, 'so I've made up this basket of good things.'

Inside the basket was a jar of honey, and a honeycomb from the hive, some fresh cream from the cow, six brown speckled eggs from the hen, a little pat of butter, and a loaf of bread, still warm from the baker. They were all neatly packed round with sweet lavender, and her mother had covered the basket with a checked cloth.

'Now,' said Little Red Riding Hood's mother. 'I want you to take this over to Granny this morning. This will set her right in no time, and seeing you will really cheer her up. But mind you stay on the path in the forest, and don't talk to anyone you don't know.'

Little Red Riding Hood promised, and then she put on her cape, picked up the basket, kissed her mother goodbye, and set off on the path into the forest.

After a little while she saw a woodcutter at work. 'Hello, Little Red Riding Hood,' he called out cheerily.

'Off to see your granny, eh? Well, mind how you go, and watch your step.'

A while later, she met a cunning and hungry wolf. He had dressed himself in a forester's green coat and breeches, and was leaning against a tree.

'Good morning, little girl,' he said very politely. 'What's your name?' But all the while he was thinking what a delicious meal she would make.

'Good morning,' said Little Red Riding Hood, not much liking the look of him. 'I'm called Little Red Riding Hood,' and she tried to walk past on the narrow path.

'Ooh, not so fast,' said the wolf, putting out a grey paw. 'What's in the pretty basket?' And he lifted the cloth, and saw all the good things underneath. 'Mmmm, delicious,' he said. 'Who are these for?'

'They are for my granny,' said Little Red Riding Hood, 'who isn't very well. She lives just over there.' Little Red Riding Hood pointed through the dark tangle of trees to where Granny's cottage could just be seen through the branches.

'Well,' said the wolf, slyly, 'don't you think dear Granny deserves some flowers as well?' And he pointed to a dell in the forest, some way from the path, where bluebells were growing.

'I suppose it couldn't do any harm,' said Little Red Riding Hood, and she skipped off the path to pick a big bunch of bluebells.

The wolf set off at once down the path to Granny's cottage. He tapped lightly on the door.

'Who's there?' Granny called out from her cosy bedroom.

'It's me, Little Red Riding Hood, Granny. I've brought you a lovely basket of good things to eat,' said the wolf in a little voice.

'You'll have to let yourself in, dear. I'm not feeling too well,' said Granny.

So the cunning wolf lifted the latch, and let himself in. He slipped into Granny's bedroom and, before she could cry out for help, swallowed her in one big gulp. Next the wolf tore off the forester's coat, put on Granny's nightcap and dressing-gown, and set himself up in bed. He pulled the cap low down over his eyes, and pulled the covers close up to his chin, so that only a tiny bit of him was showing, and then he waited.

It was not long before there came a gentle tap-tapping at the door. 'Who is it?' the wolf called out in a croaky voice.

'It's me, Granny, Little Red Riding Hood. I've brought some flowers and a basket of good things to eat.'

'Mmmm,' said the wolf, licking his lips, 'I love good things to eat. Just lift the latch and let yourself in.'

Little Red Riding Hood let herself in, and went through to the bedroom. There she saw Granny tucked up in bed looking much worse than she had imagined. She went closer and sat by the bed.

'My goodness, Granny,' she said, 'what big eyes you have.'

'All the better to see you with, my dear,' said the wolf.

'And, Granny, what big ears you have,' said Little Red Riding Hood.

'All the better to hear you with, my dear,' said the wolf.

'And most of all, what big teeth you have,' said Little Red Riding Hood.

'All the better to eat you with, my dear!' cried the wolf, and he leapt out of Granny's bed.

'Help!' screamed Little Red Riding Hood. 'Help! Help!'

The wolf, now on all fours, snarled and snapped at her heels as he chased her round and round the little bedroom. But at that moment the door burst open, and there stood the woodcutter with his axe.

He struck one great blow, and the wolf split open and out tumbled poor Granny, safe and whole, but very upset.

Later, Little Red Riding Hood gave her granny the basket of good things, and the big bunch of bluebells. Her granny loved the flowers but hoped that in future Little Red Riding Hood would always stay on the path, because the forest was such a dangerous place.

They all had a delicious meal, and then the woodcutter saw Little Red Riding Hood home. But on the way he reminded her never to talk to strangers again.

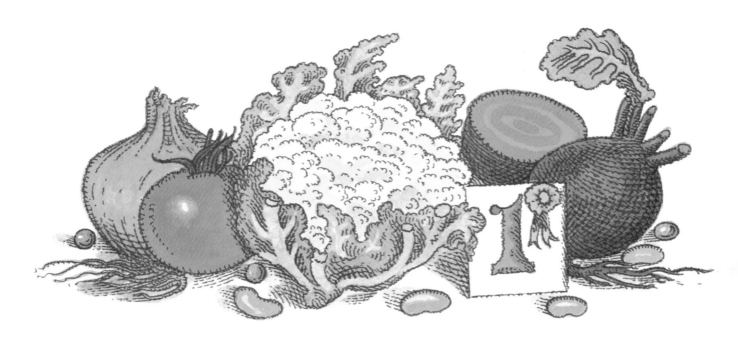

The *Giant Turnip*

Once upon a time, there was a little old man. He had a fine garden, where he grew all kinds of vegetables. He looked after his vegetables and treated them very kindly. He hoed the ground, and he kept the earth free from weeds and slugs. Everyone in the village said that his were the finest vegetables, best for colour, and best for flavor.

Now, the little old man had a secret. When all his seeds were planted and the little seedlings were just popping their heads out of the ground, he would talk to them. And this is what he would say:

'Come on, you little seedlings, grow, grow.' He said it over and over, every evening before he went to bed.

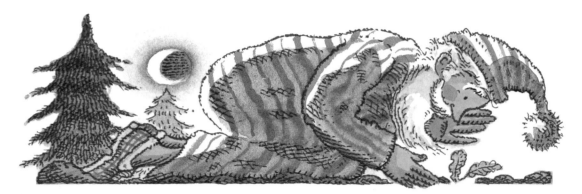

His wife would shake her head and say that he was a fool, no good could come of talking to vegetables. She said that it was her careful watering that gave them such a fine crop.

One day the little old man planted out some turnips. His wife watered them well, and in time up popped the seedlings. 'Grow, little seedlings, grow,' said the old man, and grow they did.

One of them grew much bigger than the rest. It kept on growing, and growing, until it took up a whole corner of the garden. Every morning the old man would come out and look at his turnip, he would give it a little pat, and talk kindly to it. The turnip kept on growing, until it took up half the garden.

One morning his wife said, 'It's time to pull up that gert turnip, there's enough there to feed the whole village.'

So the old man went out and began to pull up the giant turnip. He pulled and pulled, but it wouldn't move. The old man called out to his wife, and his wife came and she pulled at the old man, and the old man pulled at the turnip, but it wouldn't move.

So the wife fetched a boy who lived nearby, and the boy pulled at the wife, and the wife pulled at the old man, and the old man pulled at the turnip, but still it would not move.

So the boy went to fetch his little sister, and the sister pulled at the boy, and the boy pulled at the wife, and the wife pulled at the old man, and the old man pulled at the turnip, but still it would not move.

So the little sister ran to fetch her dog, and the dog pulled at the little sister, and the little sister pulled at the boy, and the boy pulled at the wife, and the wife pulled at the old man, and the old man pulled at the turnip, but still it would not move.

So then the dog was sent to fetch his friend the cat, and then the cat pulled at the dog, and the dog pulled at the little sister, and the little sister pulled at the boy, and the boy pulled at the wife, and the wife pulled at the old man, and the old man pulled at the turnip, but still it would not move.

So then the cat was sent to fetch her friend the little mouse, and then the little mouse pulled at the cat, and the cat pulled at the dog, and the dog pulled at the little sister, and the little sister pulled at the boy, and the boy pulled at the wife, and the wife pulled at the old man, and the old man pulled at the turnip.

Whooosh! The turnip burst out of the ground and the old man fell on the wife, the wife fell on the boy, the boy fell on the little sister, the little sister fell on the dog, the dog fell on the cat, and the cat fell on the little mouse, who said 'Eeek!'

After they all brushed themselves down, they set to and made a great feast with the giant turnip, and the whole village joined in and made a party of it.

The *Story* of the *Elves* and the *Shoemaker*

Once upon a time, when the world was young and snow fell every winter, there lived a shoemaker and his wife. He was a fine craftsman, but recently trade had not been good, and they were very poor—so much so that the shoemaker had only one piece of leather left in his workshop, enough to make just one pair of shoes. So, that evening, he sat in his cold workshop and cut out the pieces of leather into all the shapes needed to make a pair of shoes.

Then his wife called him in for their supper, and so he wearily left all the cut-out pieces on his bench ready to make up in the morning.

He and his wife made a poor supper together of watery cabbage soup and scraps, and then, with their last stub of candle, lit their way to bed.

When the shoemaker opened his workshop door in the morning he had the shock of his life. There on the bench, instead of the cut-out patterns of leather, stood as fine a pair of shoes as he had ever seen. At first he suspected a trick. He looked under the bench for the bits of leather, but there was nothing, everything was just as tidy and spare as always. He called to his wife to come, and he fetched his glass lens that he sometimes used for especially close work. Together they looked at the shoes. It was his leather all right.

'Made by a master hand, much finer than my own,' he said. 'Even my old teacher couldn't make stitches so small and neat. But where are they from?'

'No matter,' said his wife. ''Tis divine providence. These shoes will make our fortune, you'll see.' So saying, she put the shoes in the middle of the shop window.

It was not long before the shoes were noticed. A customer came in and tried them on. Walking up and down the shop, he said they were the most comfortable and handsome shoes he had ever worn, and he happily paid twice the normal price for them. Now there was enough money to buy leather to make two pairs of shoes, and even some left over for a good supper.

That evening, the shoemaker cut out the leather and left the pieces ready for making up in the morning; and that night the soup was thicker and tastier, and the shoemaker and his wife went to bed well satisfied. And sure enough, in the morning, when the shoemaker opened his workshop, there were two pairs of perfectly made shoes, all complete with their tiny stitching, and the leather soft and glossy with polish.

The shoes were soon sold, and the shoemaker was able to buy enough leather to make four pairs of shoes. Again the shoemaker carefully cut out the patterns, and again in the morning there stood four more pairs of exquisite shoes, and so it went on.

The shoemaker was able to buy more and more leather in all the colors of the rainbow. He cut out a great variety of shoes, and pumps, and slippers, and boots. Every morning he would come in to find them all perfectly finished as before.

He was soon thought to be the best shoemaker in the land, and one morning the king himself arrived with his page and chancellor and bought an especially fine pair of high boots in green leather.

One night the shoemaker and his wife could contain their curiosity no longer. They decided to hide themselves in the workshop and keep watch, just to see what sort of providence was at work. They left a tall candle lit near a pile of recently cut patterns on the workbench, and then settled in their hiding place to wait.

When the clock chimed midnight a pair of strange little figures climbed up on to the workbench. They were tiny, not much bigger than a shoe themselves, and they wore very odd clothes: acorn halves for hats, leaves and grasses and scraps for clothes. 'Elves,' whispered the shoemaker. But his wife shushed him and they settled to watch the elves at work.

The elves worked hard and fast, they stitched with tiny needles, and hammered with tiny hammers, and buffed and polished with little cloths. They worked on as the clock chimed the night hours. They didn't stop until the candle was almost burnt down and daylight showed through the frosty window. Then the two elves scuttled back under the door, leaving a line of beautiful shoes on the bench.

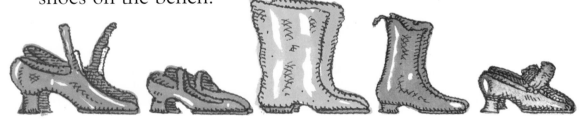

The shoemaker and his wife crept out of their hiding place. 'Did you ever see anything like it?' said the shoemaker. 'Those elves have helped us to make our fortune. And did you see what they were wearing? Just little scraps, and acorns, and bits and bobs. They must be frozen in this weather.' And the shoemaker and his wife shook their heads.

'I have an idea,' said the shoemaker's wife. 'We shall make some fine clothes for them, as a way of saying thank you.'

So, during the day, (which was Christmas Eve), the shoemaker and his wife cut and sewed with their nimble fingers. They made some little shirts, and waistcoats, and jackets, and breeches, and even stockings and mittens. They used pieces of brocade, and velvet, and

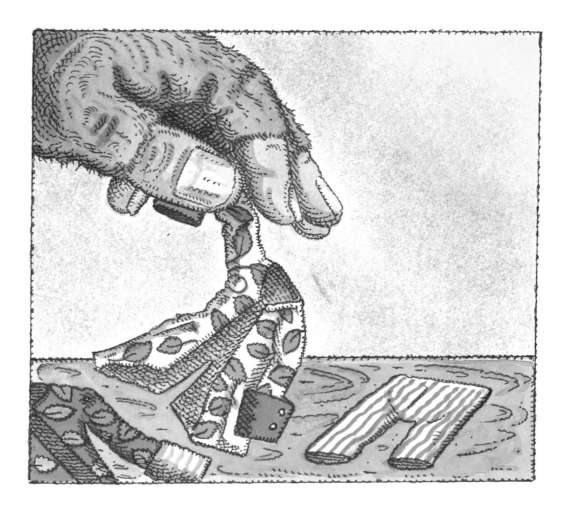

silk, and cambric, and fine wool. That night they laid out all the little clothes on the workbench, and settled themselves in their hiding place to wait.

Sure enough, as the clock chimed midnight the two elves appeared. They climbed up to the workbench, where they found all the fine new clothes, beautifully cut and sewn. The elves happily put on their new clothes, laughing and chattering to themselves.

'Happy Christmas, little men,' whispered the shoemaker and his wife.

Then the elves danced round the candlestick, and as they danced they sang,

Now we're dressed so fine and neat
We'll no more work for other's feet.

And then they danced off the bench, under the door, and were never seen again.

The shoemaker and his wife hung a smart new sign on the front of their shop; it was cut out in the shape of an elegant shoe, and had 'By Royal Appointment' painted on it in crisp gold letters. The shoemaker and his wife lived happily and prospered until the end of their days, which was a very long time indeed.

The Gingerbread Boy

Once upon a time and a long time ago, there lived an old man and an old woman. They were very sad because they had no children of their own. One morning the old woman had a good idea. She decided to make them a little boy out of gingerbread. She prepared the dough, shaped it, pressed it, kneaded it, and carefully cut out the shape of their own little boy.

She put two raisins for his eyes, and one for his nose, and he had three little buttons on his front made out of hard candy. The final touch was to draw a cheeky smile on his face with the handle of a spoon, then she called her husband in to see the little lad.

'What a fine boy,' said the husband, and together they popped him in the hot oven to bake.

When it was time to take him out they opened the oven door, and out he jumped, cheeky smile and all, their own little gingerbread boy! They looked on in astonishment as he ran across the kitchen floor and out through the open door into the street. The old couple chased after him, calling out, 'Stop, stop, come back, you're our little gingerbread boy.'

But the little gingerbread boy ran on with his cheeky grin, and he called back to them:

'Run, run, as fast as you can.
You can't catch me,
I'm the gingerbread man.'

And the poor old man and old woman really couldn't run fast enough to catch him.

On and on ran the little gingerbread boy, out of the town and into the countryside, far across the fields, until he came to a cow.

'Moo,' said the cow. 'Moo. Stop, little gingerbread boy, I want to eat you all up.'

But the little gingerbread boy ran on and shouted back to the cow, 'I can run faster than the old man and the old woman, and I can run faster than you.

'Run, run, as fast as you can.
You can't catch me,
I'm the gingerbread man.'

And the cow couldn't run fast enough to catch him.

On and on, even faster, ran the little gingerbread boy, until he met a horse. 'Neigh, neigh,' said the horse. 'Stop, little gingerbread boy. I'm hungry and you look good enough to eat.'

But the little gingerbread boy ran on past the horse, and as he ran he called out, 'I can run faster than the old man and the old woman, and a cow, and I can run much faster than you.

'Run, run, as fast as you can.
You can't catch me,
I'm the gingerbread man.'

And even the horse wasn't fast enough to catch him.

On and on, faster and faster, ran the little gingerbread boy, until he came to a farmer cutting corn.

'Hey, you!' called the farmer. 'Little gingerbread boy, stop. You're just what I need to eat for my tea.'

But the little gingerbread boy just dashed between the farmer's boots and said, 'I can run faster than the old man and the old woman, and a cow, and a horse, and I can run faster than you, too.

'Run, run, as fast as you can.
You can't catch me,
I'm the gingerbread man.'

The farmer dropped his scythe, and ran off after the little gingerbread boy, but he just couldn't run fast enough. On and on, faster and faster and faster, ran the little gingerbread boy, until he came to a river, where he had to stop. A fox was slinking past. He saw the gingerbread boy, and was suddenly very hungry. He was a cunning fox, and he had a plan.

'Why don't I help you, little gingerbread boy?' he said through shining white teeth. 'Hop on my tail, and I'll swim you over to the other side, before the farmer catches up with both of us.'

And so the little gingerbread boy, with his cheeky grin, jumped on to the fox's tail, and together they set off across the water.

After a moment the fox said, 'You seem to be getting wet. Why not jump further up my back, where you will be dry?' So the little gingerbread boy jumped up on to the fox's back.

They were nearly half-way across the river when the fox said, 'You're quite heavy on my back, little boy, why not hop up on to my nose?' So the little gingerbread boy hopped on to the fox's nose.

When they finally reached the other side of the river the fox flipped his head, snapped open his mouth, and, crunch, a quarter of the little gingerbread boy was gone.

'Oh dear,' said the little gingerbread boy.

Crunch, went the fox's jaws again, and half of the little gingerbread boy was gone.

'Oh dear, dear,' said the little gingerbread boy.

The fox snapped his jaws again and three quarters of the little gingerbread boy was gone.

'Oh dear, dear, dear,' said the little gingerbread boy.

Crunch, went the white teeth for the last time, and the little gingerbread boy, with his cheeky grin, was completely gone.

The Story of the Good and Clever Little Red Hen

Once upon a time, in a land over the sea, there lived in the same house three good friends: a cockerel, a mouse, and a little red hen. Their house nestled under a tree, at the top of a steep wooded hill. The little red hen looked after her friends all day long. She cooked, she cleaned, she tidied, she washed, and she sewed, so that everything in the little house was bright and neat and tidy . . . shipshape, and Bristol fashion.

Far below the wooded hill, across a river, was another house. Dark and dirty and hidden under the earth. A vixen fox lived there with her cubs. The little foxes cried all the time, they were so hungry. The mother fox said, 'Instead of crying all the time, you might build up a good fire, put the big pot on to boil, and lay up the table, because I am going out to catch some good supper.' And so saying, the mother fox picked up her hunting sack and slipped out of the dark little home, and made her way carefully across the river and up the wooded hill where she had scented good things to eat.

At the top of the hill in the bright little house where the cockerel and the mouse and the little red hen lived, it was breakfast time. As usual the little red hen was busy and bustling, putting on her pinafore apron with all its useful pockets. 'Now then,' she said brightly,

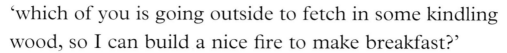

'which of you is going outside to fetch in some kindling wood, so I can build a nice fire to make breakfast?'

'Not me,' said the mouse, with a lazy yawn.

'Not me,' said the cockerel gruffly.

'Oh well,' said the little red hen, 'I'll just have to fetch it myself.'

So off she went and fetched a great bundle of kindling wood. Then she set to and made a merry fire in the kitchen range.

'Now then,' said the little red hen, 'which one of you two is going to pop out to the well and fetch me up a nice bucket of water for our tea?'

'Not me,' yawned the mouse.

'Not me,' snapped the cockerel.

'Oh well,' said the little red hen, 'I'll just have to do it myself.'

So off she flapped, out to the well, and brought back a heavy bucket of fresh water. Then the little red hen made a good breakfast of porridge, and strong tea, and lots of toast and butter and marmalade.

After breakfast the little red hen said, 'Now, which of you two is going to clear away the breakfast things so that I can wash up?'

'Not me,' said the mouse, yawning and rubbing his full tummy.

'Not me,' said the cockerel crossly. 'Not my turn.'

'Oh well,' said the little red hen brightly, 'I'll just have to do it myself.' And so she tidied away, and washed and dried all the plates and cups and spoons and pans, until the kitchen shone.

'Now,' said the little red hen after she had finished, 'who'll pop upstairs and make the beds?'

'Not me,' said the mouse from one comfy chair.

'Not me,' said the rooster from the other comfy chair.

'Oh, well then,' said the little red hen, 'I'll have to do

it myself.

So off she went up the twisty stairs to the bedrooms, while the mouse and the rooster settled back in their chairs for a well-earned rest.

A moment later came a loud knock-knocking at the door.

'I wonder who that can be,' yawned the mouse.

'Where's the little red hen?' snapped the rooster. 'It's her turn to go to the door.'

'She's upstairs,' said the mouse. 'I suppose *I* must go.'

'Yes, you must,' said the rooster. 'Because *I'm* fast asleep!'

So the mouse opened the door, and there was the vixen with her sharp teeth and her sack. 'Eeek!' squeaked the mouse, but too late. She grabbed him up and popped him in her sack.

'Who was it?' asked the rooster grumpily.

'Me,' hissed the vixen.

The startled rooster opened his eyes and began to call out 'Cock a doodle—' but before he could finish he too was stuffed into the vixen's dark sack. The little red hen came fussing down the stairs to see what all the noise was. The vixen easily popped her into the sack too.

The vixen was very pleased with her catch. She tightened a rope around the neck of the sack and set off down the hill on her long journey home. Inside the sack the three friends were very frightened.

'Oh dear, I wish I hadn't been so lazy,' said the mouse.

'Oh dear, I wish I hadn't been so lazy, *and* so cross,' said the rooster.

'Oh well,' said the little red hen, 'I expect I'll have to think of something.'

Meanwhile, the vixen carried on down the hill with her heavy load. The sun was high, and it was a hot day, and so the vixen decided to settle in the shade of a tree for a rest.

'Now then,' said the little red hen, 'here's our chance. We've stopped moving. The fox must be resting.' She took a little pair of scissors from one of her useful apron pockets, and cut a neat hole in the sack, and the three friends slipped out. 'Now,' she whispered, 'who'll fetch some stones to weigh the sack down?'

'Me,' said the mouse.

'Me,' said the rooster.

And so they both went and fetched three heavy stones and put them in the sack through the neat hole. Then the little red hen took a needle and thread from another pocket in her apron and sewed up the hole so carefully and nimbly that you would never know there had been a hole at all.

Then the three friends ran back up the hill as fast as they could to their cosy little home.

The vixen woke at sunset and hefted the sack back on to her shoulder. It felt heavier than ever—what a feast they would have later. She reached the river as the moon rose, and started to swim to the other side. The sack of stones would not float, and their weight pulled the vixen under the dark water to the bottom. The little cubs would have to wait a long time for any supper at all.

Things certainly changed up at the cosy house on the hill. Now it was the clever little red hen who sat in the comfy chair, while the rooster and the mouse did all the busy housework and cooking. And so it was to be for the rest of their lives, which was as long a time as you can imagine.

The *True Story* of
the *Three Little Pigs* and
the *Big Bad Wolf*

Once upon a time, and a long time ago, and far away, lived a mother pig, with her three little pigs. They lived happily together, but the mother pig was very poor, and three little pigs need a lot of feeding. So she decided to send them out into the world to seek their fortunes.

The three little pigs set off in the bright sunshine. Each carried his few treasures and some carrot or turnip tops, wrapped up in spotted handkerchiefs tied to sticks. Their mother bade them a tearful farewell as they made their way up the road.

After a while they reached a crossroad, and each of the little pigs set off on a different path.

The first little pig made a happy lunch of his scraps and water. Then he set off and after a little while he met a man carrying a large bundle of straw. 'Excuse me, sir,' said the little pig, 'but I wonder if you would give me that bundle of straw, so that I may build a house?'

The man said, 'Certainly, young pig. This straw is so itchy it keeps making me sneeze . . . Achoooo!' So the man happily gave the pig the straw and went on his way.

The little pig spent some happy moments building his house of straw. He set out his few treasures, and settled down to his new life.

It was not long before there was a knock at the door. 'Who's there?' asked the little pig, in a worried voice.

'It's me . . . your friend . . . the wolf . . .' came a growly reply. 'Won't you let me come in?'

'NO,' said the little pig. 'Not by the hair on my chinny-chin-chin, you shall never come in.'

'Very well,' said the wolf. 'Then I shall *huff*, and I shall *puff*, and I shall *BLOW* your house in.'

So the wolf huffed and he puffed, and he blew down the little straw house with a great gale of wolf's breath. While the dust and straw whirled around, the little pig ran off as fast as he could across the fields.

The second little pig had carried on up his chosen road. After a while, he too had made a simple lunch of turnip tops. Later, he too had met a man. He was carrying a big bundle of sticks.

'Excuse me, sir,' asked the pig politely, 'I wonder if you would give me that bundle of sticks so that I may build myself a house?'

'Of course, little pig, since you ask so nicely,' replied the man. He was only too glad to give the bundle of sticks away. He had been carrying them so long, that he had forgotten why he had them in the first place.

So the second little pig built a house with the sticks. He too settled down happily with his few treasures. But it wasn't long before there was a very quiet tap tap on the door. 'Who is it?' asked the little pig, nervously.

'It's me. Your brother,' said a worried little voice. 'Oh, do let me in. Please hurry!' So the second little pig opened the door, and in fell his brother. He was breathless and panting hard, and just as he was about to speak, there came a loud knock-knocking at the door.

'Who's there?' asked the little pigs.

'Cooeee . . . it's me . . . the wolf . . .' growled a sly voice. 'Why not open the door and let me in?'

'No!' cried the two little pigs. 'Never, not by the hairs on our chinny-chin-chin-chins, you shall never come in!'

'Very well,' said the wolf. 'Then I shall *huff* and I shall *puff*, and I shall *BLOW* your house down.' So the wolf huffed and he puffed, a great smelly gale of wolf breath, and the house of sticks blew apart. Out of the swirl of sticks and dust the two little pigs ran as fast as they could.

Now the third little pig had done exactly the same as his brothers. He had walked happily through the warm afternoon. He had stopped by a stream to eat his picnic of scraps. Later, on the road, he had met a man. This man was pulling a cart laden with heavy bricks and bags of cement.

'Excuse me, sir,' enquired the polite pig, 'but I wonder if you might spare me those bricks and some of that cement? They are just what I need to build myself a safe little house.'

'Why, I should be glad to, young pig,' said the man. 'Pulling this load is hard work in this hot weather.'

So the third little pig spent some happy hours building his little house of brick. When he had finished it was very neat, with four square walls, and topped out with a fine chimney.

He had no sooner settled down inside than there came a tap-tapping at his door.

'Who's there?' he asked.

'It's us. Your brothers. Oh, do please let us in.'

So the little pig opened his door, and in they tumbled. One was covered in bits of straw and the other was covered in bits of stick, and both looked the worse for wear. They were very out of breath. They had just started to gather themselves to speak when there came a loud knock-knocketty-knock-knock, on the door.

'Who's there?' said the little pigs.

'It's me. . .the wolf. . .' growled out a gruff and hungry voice. 'Why not just open the door and let me in?'

'Never!' cried out the little pigs. 'Not by every single hair on our chinny-chin-chin-chin-chinny-chins . . . you shall never come in.'

'Oh, very well,' said the wolf, 'if you must. Then I shall *huff* and I shall *puff*, and I shall *BLOW* your house down . . . and then I shall come in and eat you all up!'

And so the wolf drew in all his breath. Then he huffed. Then he puffed, a great hurricane of wolf breath at the little brick house. But when he had finished the little house was still there. So again the wolf puffed and huffed, huffed and puffed, until he could blow no more. And still the little house stood firm.

By now the wolf was worn out with all the huffing and puffing. He was hungry, and he was cross. He could see the three little pigs watching him from the window. He snarled at them . . . 'I shall find another way in.' The wolf began to climb on to the roof of the little brick house.

'He means to come down the chimney,' said the first little pig.

'Oh, help! What shall we do . . .?' said the second little pig.

'I know what we must do,' said the third little pig. 'We must build a good fire in my fireplace.'

So the three little pigs set to with a will and soon had a good fire blazing.

The wolf, being very lean and very hungry, was able to lower himself down the narrow chimney, bottom first. As his bottom inched downwards, so the flames and heat from the fire inched upwards . . . until suddenly . . . 'Yowlllll!' The wolf's bottom and tail were properly scorched and he shot sparking out of the chimney like a rocket.

The three little pigs were never troubled by the wolf again. They continued to live happily in the safe little brick house. They grew carrots and turnips. Soon they were rich enough to send for their mother to live with them. And they all lived happily together for as long as they could. Which was a very long time.

Goldilocks and the Three Bears

O nce upon a time, and a long time ago, there was a little girl called Goldilocks. She lived in a wooden house on the edge of a forest. Her father was a woodcutter, and he worked deep among the tall trees. Every morning, Goldilocks would take him some fresh bread and a hot drink to where he worked. It was a big forest, full of pathways that led this way and that. Goldilocks liked to explore the paths that led through the forest, but her father warned her to be careful, because one day her curiosity would land her in trouble.

So it was early one morning, when Goldilocks set off down a path she had never seen before. At the end of the path she came to a cosy little house, made of rough-cut logs. It had shutters over the windows with strange bear-shaped holes cut in them. She crept up close to a window and, standing on tip-toe, peeped in. She could see a very warm-looking kitchen, with a good fire going, and a merry kettle on the boil.

'I wonder who lives here?' she whispered to herself. 'It couldn't do any harm just to creep in and see.' So very quietly she lifted the latch and went in.

In the kitchen there was a shelf, with a row of honey jars; some big, some middle sized, and some very small.

Whoever lives here likes honey, she thought. It was warm in the kitchen, and there was a lovely smell of fresh porridge. In the middle of the kitchen, on a solid wooden table, she found three bowls.

Goldilocks, who was very hungry because she had had no breakfast, said, 'It couldn't do any harm just to have a little taste, it smells so good.' So she tried some porridge from the first bowl, which was very big, but . . . oh no . . . that was too hot. So she tried some porridge from the next bowl, which was middle sized, but . . . ugh . . . that porridge was too cold. So next she tried the porridge in the third bowl, which was tiny wee, and that porridge was . . . mmmmmm . . . just right, and so she had another taste, and another, until all the porridge was gone.

After so much porridge Goldilocks thought that it would do no harm just to have a little sit down. There were three chairs.

She tried sitting on the first chair, which was very big, but was not comfortable. So she tried the second chair, which was middle sized, but no . . . that wasn't comfortable either. So then she sat on the third chair, which was tiny wee, and that felt . . . mmmmm . . . just right. But she had only sat on it for a moment when suddenly the legs gave way and fell into pieces, and she landed with a bump on the floor.

Goldilocks picked herself up, and thought that after all that porridge and sitting, she was very tired. What she needed was a nice lie down. It couldn't do any harm just to have a peep upstairs at the bedroom. So very carefully and quietly, she crept up the twisty stairs.

Upstairs in the bedroom Goldilocks found three beds.

She tried lying down on the first bed, which was very big. But she just couldn't get comfortable. So then she tried the second bed which was middle sized. She lay on that for a moment, but she couldn't get comfortable there either. And so she lay on the third bed which was tiny wee, and that felt . . . mmmm . . . very comfortable, and she thought, It couldn't do any harm to lie under this nice cover for a little while. Because of course she was very tired from eating all that porridge, sitting on all those chairs, and climbing all the way up the twisty stairs to the bedroom. And so she yawned, snuggled up against the pillow, and fell fast asleep.

As Goldilocks fell asleep, the owners of the little house came back from their walk. They had been walking round and round the forest, because their breakfast porridge was too hot. They were looking forward to it being just right and to stirring some lovely honey into it. They were very fond of honey because they were bears.

There were three of them. There was a daddy bear, who was very, very, big. There was a mummy bear, who was middle sized. And there was a baby bear, who was tiny wee. The big daddy bear looked into his bowl of porridge with a happy smile. Now it would be just right. But then his expression changed. First he looked puzzled. Then he looked cross. 'Somebody has been eating my porridge,' he boomed.

The middle-sized mummy bear looked into her bowl of porridge. 'Oh dear,' she cried, 'somebody has been eating my porridge, too.'

The tiny wee baby bear held up his bowl and said, 'Somebody has been eating my porridge . . . and it's all gone.'

Then the big daddy bear sat down, plomp, in his big chair . . . and then jumped up again. 'Why, somebody has been sitting in my chair,' he thundered.

Then the middle-sized mummy bear sat down in her chair and said, 'Someone has been sitting in my chair, too.'

The tiny wee baby bear went to sit in his little chair, only to fall, bump, on his bottom . . .

'Oooh! Somebody sat in my chair,' he cried, 'and now it's all broken.'

The big daddy bear thought for a moment, and said, 'Someone has been in here.'

The middle-sized mummy bear thought for a moment and said, 'They might still be here.'

The tiny wee baby bear thought for a moment and said, 'Someone's been up the stairs.'

The three bears made their way carefully up the twisty stair to the bedroom. The big daddy bear looked at his bed. 'Somebody has been sleeping in my bed,' he growled.

The middle-sized mummy bear looked at her bed. 'Somebody has been sleeping in my bed, too,' she whispered.

The tiny wee baby bear looked at his bed. 'And somebody has been sleeping in my bed . . . and they are still here.' He jumped up and down and pointed to the head of golden curls on his pillow.

The big daddy bear went up to the tiny wee bed. He leaned over and very gently tapped Goldilocks on the shoulder.

Goldilocks sat up in bed, stretched out her arms, yawned, and then saw the three bears standing round the tiny bed. She saw a great big bear, and a middle-sized bear, and a tiny wee bear who smiled at her.

'Little girl,' said the big daddy bear, 'did you eat our porridge?'

'Yes, I did,' said Goldilocks in a scared whisper. 'I didn't think it would do any harm.'

'And did you sit on our chairs?' said the middle-sized mummy bear.

'And break one?' said the tiny wee baby bear.

'Yes, I did,' whispered Goldilocks. 'I didn't mean to do any harm. I'm very sorry.'

'Well, never mind,' said the middle-sized mummy bear. 'You come downstairs with us, we've none of us had our porridge yet.'

They all went down the twisty stair to the cosy kitchen. They had fresh bowls of porridge. The mummy bear was surprised that Goldilocks had room in her tummy for any more porridge.

Goldilocks sat on the middle-sized chair. The tiny wee baby bear said, 'You broke my chair.' So Goldilocks put the baby bear on her lap.

The mummy bear said, 'Whenever you want to have some porridge with us you are very welcome, but you should ask first.' The big daddy bear nodded his head.

When Goldilocks said goodbye, she took away the pieces of broken chair with her for her father to mend. After that she often visited the little house deep in the forest for porridge. And, of course, to play with the tiny wee baby bear.

I have tried to retell these familiar old stories in much the same way that I used to tell them to my own children at bedtime, although without perhaps going as far as draping an old coat over my head and tapping on the bedroom door as a scary wolf, which I was regularly forced to do, along with making all the right growls and squeaks. I did however rescue the three little pigs, one by one, because my daughter wanted me to. In any case the drawings have to make the growls and squeaks instead.

Some of the stories I chose because of the opportunity they gave for drawing the pictures. I had always wanted to draw Little Red Riding Hood as a splash of scarlet in a grey-green forest, or Goldilocks being discovered by the three bears. I chose 'The Little Red Hen' because it seemed only too like the life around me. The red hen's friends, the cockerel and the mouse, seem exactly like two teenage boys complaining that it is always somebody else's turn to do the slightest domestic chore.

In some stories I have also wilfully mixed things up, for the sake of making an interesting picture, so that Jack flies away from the giant on the back of the goose that lays the golden eggs, and Goldilocks, instead of running away from the three bears, befriends them instead, and ends by playing badminton with the tiny wee bear, which I felt was just what she should do.

Ian Beck
London, 1998